OLD MAN OF THE NORTH

Joy Allardyce

Illustrator Scott Webb

First published 2023 by MRW Publishing
Copyright © 2023 Joy Allardyce

ISBN
Paperback - 978-0-6453330-6-0
eBook - 978-0-6453330-5-3

MRW Publishing acknowledges the Traditional Owners and their custodianship of the lands on which MRW Publishing operates. We pay our respects to their Ancestors and their descendants, who continue cultural and spiritual connections to Country. We recognise their valuable contributions to Australian and global society.

Scott Webb grants permission to Joy Allardyce to use and reproduce the artwork images which are subject to copyright.

Cover Image: Scott Webb   Nim's Journey to the Bay
Back Cover Image: Scott Webb   Nim and Naluma's final journey; coming together, connected in One Place
Book Design: MRW Publishing
Graphic Artist: Lindy Reger

MRW Publishing
Brisbane,
Queensland, Australia 4001
www.tracytully.com

OLD MAN OF THE NORTH

Joy Allardyce is an international bestselling author.
She has written and published several short stories in regional
newspapers across Australia, raising her three girls as her family
travelled.
Old Man of the North was published while living in Toowoomba,
southeast Queensland.

OTHER BOOKS BY JOY ALLARDYCE

Come Fly with Me ... on a DC-3

DEDICATION

To Lindy, Tracy, and Caroline,
my daughters and my friends.

ARTIST - Scott Webb

My name is Scott Webb I am a Dharawal born Aboriginal man, I am also recognised from the Dharug and Gundungurra people and have connections to and respect the traditional custodians of the central desert Anangu people (PY Lands).

I have been a recognised registered Aboriginal artist for over 16 years. I am a registered and recognised Aboriginal artist with Indigenous Art Code and Aboriginal Art Association of Australia.

From living in Central Australia, North Coast, South Coast NSW, Central West New South Wales, and Southwest Queensland, I have worked with many diverse artists from different communities and styles, developing my own style of storytelling through traditional art.

I express my art through different Disciplines which include dot painting on canvas, digital art, wood, and ceramics also sculpture with wood ceramics and other T-shirts, rugby jerseys, clothing and making traditional tools.

My art is my identity, all my art has a story for connection to culture and knowledge, and it's a belonging. It's Family and Lore.

I give permission and ownership of these two pieces of my artwork purchased by: Joy Allardyce and Tracy Tully to use and reproduce the artwork which is copyrighted.

Artist Scott Webb

DESCRIPTION

Old man Nim has a compelling desire to visit his favourite place on the bay.

He wants to fish for barramundi and catch up with old friends.

Naluma, his wife, wants to accompany him. She is worried he is walking alone on the bush track.

He says, "Next time."

Joy Allardyce, 2023

OLD MAN OF THE NORTH

By the time Nim began the steep climb, the sun was a golden nugget high in the sky and the weight of its heat striking the earth, bent the old man's back. His face was furrowed like the land he trod, and perspiration blisters united like the great rivers of the north, rushing into his eyes, stinging – almost blinding him.

To make matters worse, the road was rough, studded with razor-sharp stones, dislodged by the grader, a mechanical bully that fractured the ground and tore at the trees with the strength of fifty mighty warriors.

Nim halted, puffing, and blowing through rounded lips as if to get rid of the hot air that filled his lungs. He turned, squinting into the golden glare, and looked down at the settlement spread below him.

New buildings were mushrooming everywhere and the general store, once a place for a quiet chat, seethed with people. Inside its belly of crowded confusion, shoppers jostled each other, as they ogled bulging shelves and grabbed at brightly coloured packets, while around the entrance, teenagers stamped and swayed to the beat of an alien music.

Nim grunted. "For the good of all people," several council elders had argued at the last meeting but, the old man was unconvinced. Was modern living worth sacrificing tribal customs and beliefs? Some would think so. Already men and women, whom he had known as children, no longer wanted the old way of life.

"So! This is how it will end," muttered the old man and turned his back on the spinning figures. When he reached the top, he paused to catch his breath, then loped downhill, digging his heals into the earth, using them like brakes to slow his speed.

He found his wife slumped against the trunk of a tall pine tree. She was watching the endless flow of white tipped waves, sweeping in from the ocean, and crashing onto the sand.

Squatting beside her he looked out across the bay. Far away to the north-east, billowing clouds poked plum-coloured heads above the horizon. "A thunderstorm," Nim thought to himself, "A bad month, November. This build-up of clouds before the wet, the air heavy with moisture. The swarms of sandflies, mosquitoes and always ... always the heat."

Today, however, Nim was happy to be sitting beneath the trees, feeling Naluma's shoulder touching his, smelling the fresh fragrance of the pines and listening to the movement of the sea. He could hear its thunderous rebellion, as it met the reef head-on and saw the waves, broken in their run, pounding at the obstruction. Now and then the wind snatched at the flying white spume, carrying it to where he sat. Nim licked his lips and tasted the salt.

He sneaked a glance at Naluma. "Tomorrow, I go away," he said stroking the faded crumpled skin of her arm.

"You want me to come?" she asked, without turning.

"No! This time, I go alone."

Poor Naluma. During the past few weeks, arthritis had turned her into a drone-pipe, which continually pursued old grievances, with the tenacity of a blood hound.

So, when Naluma shrugged her bony shoulders and murmured, "I'll wait," Nim's eyes narrowed in surprise. He should have guessed.

As Nim continued his journey, he wondered about Naluma. Perhaps he should have asked her to come too. Her snail's pace would have slowed him down, but he asked himself, would that really have mattered? Maybe he should turn back. No, he decided, he was beginning to tire, better to push on.

He was not far from his destination, when through the smoky heat haze, Nim saw a bull buffalo. What a magnificent hide, like polished stone. The beast raised its majestic head, black nostrils quivered, searching the air for the scent of man.

Nim held his breath, at the same time marveling at the size of the perfectly shaped horns. Since he was unarmed and knowing that a charge by the buffalo meant certain death, Nim left the track and with the magic of his race, disappeared into the undergrowth.

About an hour later, Nim emerged at the beach on the other side of the bay and headed for the shack. The small building squatted alone under tall Coral Gums; scattered amongst them, untidy Pandanus Palms looked up at the sky and further back, almost out of sight, stood an enormous, old Banyan tree.

As Nim collected firewood, he thought again of Naluma. He missed his wife, even missed her wagging tongue. "Yes," he said aloud, "I'll go back for her tomorrow."

After storing plenty of wood Nim returned to the shack for a spear. He strutted down to the water's edge, splashed through the shallows, and waded out to a rocky point where he knew the big fish lurked. Only when the sea clutched at his waist, did he halt, spear poised and glistening body relaxed, ready for the kill.

NALUMA

That night Naluma was visited by a soul unseen. It brushed her forehead. She stirred and murmured Nim's name, just as the last light of the moon slipped through the window and touched her face. In the dim light there hovered around her features a hint of youthful beauty, a beauty now coarsened by age, wind, and tropical sun.

What's this? Old Nim – dead? Was it by mortal whisper that she heard such a thing? Or was it a thought borne by the breeze as it skimmed the curling crests of waves?

She slept fitfully. Sometime later, she heard a burst of voices, a door creaking and padding feet swishing against the floor. They sounded as though they were close!

Suddenly, several hands grabbed her, pushing and prodding until she thought they would never stop.

"Old woman, wake up!" urged a voice. "Wake up!"

Sitting up was painful. Naluma cursed her stiff joints, then cursed the women who had interrupted her sleep.

"What you want? What you want, eh?" she demanded.

The answer came as an apology. "We come about your husband. No more can we speak his name. His spirit has left us."

"When did it happen?" she croaked, remembering the dream.

"At the peak of the dark night, old woman. Some fishermen found him on the other side of the bay."

"Go away," Naluma ordered.

The women hesitated.

"Get out!" she spat at them, and they scampered through the doorway to join the crowd of people waiting outside.

"So, it's true. He's gone!" wailed Naluma. "This is a cruel day." She pounded the bed with her fists, tears crowded her eyes and her heart felt like a thumping ball.

And now, the grief-stricken Naluma mourned the earthly Nim. "This sadness – it's too heavy for me to carry," she said to the empty room. "I'll walk to the other side of the bay, then this weary old body will be content."

As she spoke, Naluma felt a restless ache, a pain such as she had never known before. Her spirit grew impatient and soon its empty shell lay forsaken.

Naluma found the place where Nim had entered the bush and followed the path. At first, she was afraid. It had been many years since she had travelled alone. She stumbled on ignoring the branches that slapped against her chest and scratched her thighs; instead, she listened to the night birds and was comforted by the dew-wet earth, beneath her feet.

Not long after, when she staggered off the track, she met Nim. They were so happy to see each other. They walked together, talked, laughed, and held hands, until at last they reached the old Banyan tree.

As they stood beneath the towering tree, they looked up through the branches and saw the great ancestral spirits smiling down upon them. And, because the spirits were well pleased with Nim and Naluma, they showered them with blessings.

THE END

AUTHOR

Joy Allardyce

In 2019, Joy Allardyce became a first-time published book author of "Come Fly With Me … on a DC-3." She enthusiastically wrote about the early 1950s flying days of the committed air hostesses (hosties) who crewed the intrepid DC-3 while working single-handed when they didn't belong to a union!

On Armistice Day, 11th November 1930 Joy Shipway was born, and was named "Joy" to commemorate the end of World War I. Growing up in Maroubra, a suburb of Sydney, she was a keen reader early in her childhood. For nine years she belonged to a dance studio. Her routines included learning classical ballet, tap, Russian and Dutch which proved exceedingly difficult mastering the art of dancing in wooden clogs. She also had elocution, drama lessons and piano lessons and in between all of this, she squeezed in swimming lessons at Coogee Beach Rockpool.

In 1945 at the young age of fifteen, Joy successfully completed the Intermediate Certificate with seven subjects to her credit, English, General Mathematics, History (English and Australian), Geography, Physiology, Needle Work and Shorthand/Typing.

Joy's love of writing ignited her passion to be a news reporter.

After discussion with her parents seeking permission to allow her to apply for such a position, her father approached a couple of Sydney newspaper editors who were totally against the idea because Joy had only just turned fifteen years of age in the previous November.

The problem was that war correspondents were returning from the second World War (1939 – 1945) and needed to fill the positions that were available. Even though Joy would have been a cub reporter, the editors were not keen on the idea of a young girl in post-war newsrooms.

After a few tears and much deliberation, Joy then thought she would like to be an English teacher. However, this time, it was her mother who was against the idea. She ultimately became a private secretary to the Resident Liaison Engineer at General Motors Holden, where she witnessed the first Holden automobile make its Australian debut.

This position led to a top secretarial job as private secretary to the Managing Director at Otis Elevators in Sydney. At nineteen years of age, Joy reached the zenith of her career.

Joy's love of flying began in her late teens, visiting relatives at Evans Head and Nimbin on a DC-3. She remembers one trip fondly, when she carried a glass jar of six goldfish for an elderly aunt who lived in Evans Head and later, she flew again on a DC-3 to Tumut via Wagga Wagga.

In 1951, Joy won Queen of the Manly Mardi Gras. The prize was a flight to Hayman Island by a QANTAS flying boat taking off on the waters of Sydney Harbour. Her return flight home from Hayman to Sydney was on a DC-3, hence her fascination with this aircraft began.

In 1952 Joy was accepted as an air hostess with the government owned Trans-Australia Airlines (TAA).

Joy eventually became a dedicated Air Hostess crewing the intrepid TAA DC-3 aircraft in Queensland and other states during the early 1950s. She regularly meets with other ex-hosties, enjoying each other's company, sharing stories and laughs, while remembering the good old flying days.

There is a unique connection that exists between ex-hosties who never baulk at helping and supporting each other.

After her graduation, Joy was posted to Brisbane port at Eagle Farm and spent the following three years crewing mainly DC-3s, Skymaster DC-4s and Convairs across every state of Australia, including Tasmania.

After studying Professional Journalism through the Adelaide Technical College, Joy wrote and had published short stories, poems, and non-fictional narratives and in the 1970s worked for the Hedland Times, a subsidiary of the West Australian newspaper while residing in Mount Newman, Western Australia.

While living in Mount Isa in Queensland, Joy began an English course with the Queensland Secondary Correspondence School and won the Year 12 English Prize. The speech she gave on Awards Night was called "The Wonderful World of Literature."

At the age of 89, Joy had her first book published, entitled "Come Fly With Me … on a DC-3."

ACKNOWLEDGEMENTS

I was inspired to write this story by the many years I've spent living in remote and isolated areas in the Australian states of Western Australia, Northern Territory and Queensland.

While in Meekatharra, Western Australia, I worked at the school helping Indigenous children to ride horses. In Nhulunbuy, Arnhem Land, I also supported Indigenous children.

In the past, when I submitted a manuscript for perusal, it was on paper and forwarded by mail using the traditional postal system! Now the publisher receives a digital copy of the manuscript, created using the computer, and sent via electronic mail. How things have changed!

My sincere thanks to my three daughters; Tracy, my Publisher, Lindy my Graphic Artist, and Caroline my Editor. The four of us are keeping the process of book writing and publishing in the family!

My grateful and sincere thanks to Scott Webb, a talented Indigenous artist, for his vibrant works of art which are now the illustrations on my book covers.

Thank you, Scott!

Joy Allardyce

www.ingramcontent.com/pod-product-compliance
Lightning Source LLC
Chambersburg PA
CBHW042137120726
47911CB00022B/109